Katie
and the
Sunflowers

James Mayhew

ORCHARD BOOKS • NEW YORK

For Margaret
and all the children and staff at
Tacolneston Primary School, Norfolk,
~ with love and admiration ~
And for Sue, who likes sunflowers,
~ with love ~

To learn more about the postimpressionist painters, turn to the end of the book.

Copyright © 2000 by James Mayhew
First American edition 2001 published by Orchard Books
First published in Great Britain in 2000 by Orchard Books London
James Mayhew asserts the moral right to be identified as the author/illustrator of this work.

Orchard Books, A Scholastic Company, 95 Madison Avenue, New York, NY 10016

Manufactured in Belgium. Book design by Mina Greenstein. The text of this book is set in 16 point Galliard.
The illustrations are watercolor.   2 3 4 5 6 7 8 9 10

Library of Congress Cataloging-in-Publication Data
Mayhew, James, date.
Katie and the sunflowers / written and illustrated by James Mayhew.—lst American ed.   p.   cm.
Summary: While visiting the art museum, Katie has an adventure stepping in and out of five paintings by van Gogh, Gauguin, and Cézanne.
Includes information about postimpressionism and the particular paintings and artists in the story.
ISBN 0-531-30325-X (alk. paper)
[1. Museums—Fiction. 2. Postimpressionism (Art)—Fiction. 3. Art appreciation—Fiction.] I. Title.
PZ7.M4684 Kari 2000 [E]—dc21 00-32420

Grandma was helping Katie plant seeds in the garden when it started to rain.

"Never mind," Grandma said. "The rain will make everything grow."

"But what will we do instead?" said Katie.

"Let's go to the museum," said Grandma. "You always have fun there."

When they arrived, Grandma sat down to rest, so Katie went off by herself to look around. The museum was full of warm, sunny paintings. Katie liked a painting called *Sunflowers* by Vincent van Gogh.

The sunflowers looked dry and crunchy and were full of seeds.
"I would love to grow seeds like these in my garden," said
Katie. She reached into the painting and discovered she could
touch them!

But Katie bumped the vase. It wobbled and fell right out of the picture, spilling sunflowers and seeds all over the floor.

"Oh no," said Katie. "I'd better clean this up before anyone sees."

Just then Katie heard giggling.

She looked around, but there was no one else in the room. The laughter was coming from *Breton Girls Dancing* by Paul Gauguin.

"What's so funny?" said Katie, climbing inside.

Katie saw that she was standing beside a farm. The three girls—Masie, Musette, and Mimi—giggled and pointed at the mess Katie had made.

"You'll be in big trouble if anyone finds out," they said.

"Well, I didn't mean to knock over the vase," said Katie. "Will you help me clean it up?"

"Too tired," said Masie.

"We've been dancing all day," said Musette.

Katie turned to Mimi. "What about you?"

"Only if I can bring Zazou," said Mimi, picking up her dog.

"I suppose it's all right," said Katie. "Let's go."

So they went through
the frame and into the museum.

Mimi and Katie gathered up the sunflowers,
but Zazou wanted to play. He snatched the flowers
and ran off.

"How can we put the picture back together
now?" said Katie angrily.

"I'm sorry, *mon amie*," said Mimi. "Let's try to
catch him!"

They chased Zazou, but he was too quick for them. Suddenly he took a flying leap toward *Café Terrace at Night* by Vincent van Gogh and disappeared inside.

Katie and Mimi jumped in after him.

Zazou refused to let go of
the sunflowers. He darted between
tables and chairs, bumping into
them and sending plates and cups
flying.

Then he ran between the waiter's legs.

"Zut alors!" cried the waiter, dropping a plate of pastries.
He was very angry. He chased Katie, Mimi, and Zazou right
through the frame and back into the museum.

"What are we going to do?" gasped Mimi.

"I've got an idea," said Katie, spotting a painting by Paul Cézanne called *Still Life with Apples and Oranges*. "Come on, I need your help!"

Katie reached into the painting and grabbed one end of the tablecloth. She told Mimi to take the other end.

"Now pull!" yelled Katie.

The bowls of fruit tipped over, and apples and oranges came tumbling into the museum, just as the waiter caught up with them.

He slipped on the fruit and spun around till he was dizzy.

"Zut alors!" he yelled.

"I wonder where Zazou went," said Mimi.

"He must be here somewhere," said Katie as they dashed away.

"*Hélas!*" said Mimi. "I'll never find him, and he'll be lost in the museum forever."

"Wait," said Katie. "I hear a dog barking."

They followed the noise, and there at the end of the corridor was Zazou.

He had dropped the sunflowers and was barking at the bright red dog in *Tahitian Pastorals* by Paul Gauguin. The red dog barked back, and Zazou jumped inside the picture.

"Your dog is nothing but trouble," Katie grumbled as they clambered in after him.

Zazou and the red dog barked at
each other, wagging their tails.

"Welcome to our island!" said two
beautiful women.

It was very peaceful. The breezes
were full of the scent of flowers in bloom,
and the sea gently lapped the beach.

"Phew!" said Katie. "It's very hot
here. Let's go wading."

While Zazou and the red dog scampered on the beach, Katie and Mimi splashed in the sea.

Zazou was digging furiously when, all of a sudden, he disappeared.

"Where has he gone?" said Mimi.

Katie peered into the hole. It was very large, and at the bottom was Zazou, sitting on top of a big chest. Mimi and Katie moved him aside and slowly raised the lid. It was full of gold coins!

"Pirate treasure!" said Katie, showing the women. "What will you do with it?"

"We have no use for money here. We have everything we could ever need," they said. "You can have it if you'd like!"

Katie took a handful of coins and thanked the women. Then she, Mimi, and Zazou went through the frame and back into the museum.

Katie quickly picked up the sunflowers before Zazou could grab them again.

"We'd better put these back," she said. "Which way is it?"

"I'm not sure, *mon amie*," said Mimi. "I think we're lost!"

Then they saw Zazou sniffing at something on the ground.

"Sunflower seeds!" said Katie. "Zazou's left a trail of them. What a clever dog! I'm glad he came after all."

Mimi gathered Zazou up in her arms, and they followed the trail of sunflower seeds back to the Cézanne still life.

They carefully replaced the fruit and then went on to the café picture by van Gogh.

The waiter was standing there with a piece of paper in his hand.

"It's a bill," said Mimi. "For the pastries we ruined."

Katie dug into her pocket and took out the gold coins.

"Is this enough?" she asked the waiter.

"*Merci!*" he said, looking very pleased. "You may eat here whenever you want!" And he climbed back into his picture.

Katie and Mimi followed the seed trail back to the sunflower picture. Katie collected a few seeds from the floor, wrapped them in a tissue, and put them in her coat pocket. Then she carefully arranged the sunflowers in their vase and put them back in the picture.

"Almost as good as new!" said Katie. "Thanks for coming."

"I'm glad I did, *mon amie*," said Mimi. "It was fun!" And she hopped into her picture with Zazou.

Grandma was just waking up when Katie returned.

"Shall we see if it's stopped raining?" Grandma said.

It hadn't, but Katie didn't mind. "Rain is good for the garden," she said. "It will make everything grow."

The Postimpressionists

The impressionists were artists who used dabs of color to capture their impressions of contemporary life. They were followed by the postimpressionists, such as Vincent van Gogh, Paul Gauguin, and Paul Cézanne, who used color and form in a different way: they painted in thicker strokes, and their colors were even stronger. Using strong shapes and lines, postimpressionist painters tried to express their feelings through their pictures.

Vincent van Gogh (1853–1890)

Vincent van Gogh is famous for his use of color, which makes his paintings look almost alive. The paint is very thick, and the color is very bright. *Sunflowers* is a good example of this. You can see it at the National Gallery in London, England. He also painted *Café Terrace at Night,* in Arles, France, where he lived for a while. It is now in the Kröller-Müller Museum in Otterlo, the Netherlands, where van Gogh was born.

While he was alive, not many people liked his pictures, so he was often very poor. When he needed more paints, he swapped his pictures for them.

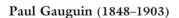

Paul Gauguin (1848–1903)

Paul Gauguin was born in France. He liked van Gogh's paintings, and they worked together for a while. They even painted pictures of each other. Gauguin painted *Breton Girls Dancing* in 1888. It's now in the National Gallery of Art in Washington, D.C.

Later Gauguin moved to Tahiti, where the tropical colors inspired him to paint in an exciting new way. *Tahitian Pastorals,* which is now in the Hermitage museum in St. Petersburg, Russia, is typical of this style. Gauguin had some sunflower seeds sent to Tahiti because sunflowers didn't grow there. Perhaps he wanted them to remind him of France and his old friend van Gogh.

Paul Cézanne (1839–1906)

Paul Cézanne was also born in France. He knew both van Gogh and Gauguin. He arranged colors and shapes very carefully, and the more he painted, the more abstract his pictures became. It took him a long time to paint a picture. If he painted people they had to sit still for many days, so it was easier to paint still lifes and landscapes. His last paintings influenced so many artists that he is called "the father of modern art." You can see *Still Life with Apples and Oranges* at the Musée d'Orsay in Paris, France.

Paintings by these three artists can be found in museums and galleries all over the world.

Acknowledgments

Sunflowers (oil on canvas) by Vincent van Gogh, © National Gallery, London, England/Bridgeman Art Library. *Breton Girls Dancing* (oil on canvas), Pont Aven, 1888, by Paul Gauguin, Richard Carafelli; © Board of Trustees, National Gallery of Art, Washington, D.C. *Café Terrace at Night,* "Place du Forum" (oil on canvas), Arles, 1888, by Vincent van Gogh, Kröller-Müller Museum, Otterlo, the Netherlands. *Still Life with Apples and Oranges* (oil on canvas), 1895–1900, by Paul Cézanne (1839–1906), Musée d'Orsay, Paris, France/Peter Willi/Bridgeman Art Library. *Pastorales Tahitiennes* (oil on canvas), 1893, by Paul Gauguin (1848–1903), Hermitage, St. Petersburg, Russia/Bridgeman Art Library.